TOY TROUBLE

by Justine Korman Fontes

Illustrated by Rob Hefferan

For all the Lost Boys and Frazzled Fairies whose
friendship brightens Neverland—J.K.F.

For my lamb—R.H.

Text copyright © 2003 by Justine Korman Fontes
Illustrations copyright © 2003 by Rob Hefferan
under exclusive license to MONDO Publishing

For information contact:
MONDO Publishing
980 Avenue of the Americas
New York, NY 10018
Visit our website at www.mondopub.com

Printed in China
03 04 05 06 07 08 09 HC 9 8 7 6 5 4 3 2 1
07 08 09 10 11 12 PB 9 8 7 6 5 4 3 2

ISBN 1-59034-446-4 (hardcover)   ISBN 1-59034-447-2 (pbk.)

Designed by Edward Miller

Library of Congress Cataloging-in-Publication Data

Korman, Justine
Toy trouble / by Justine Korman Fontes; illustrated by Rob Hefferan.
p. cm.
Summary: When Zack loses the toy he always sleeps with, Henry
and Lucy help him look for it and offer him their own.
ISBN 1-59034-446-4 -- ISBN 1-59034-447-2 (pbk.)
[1. Lost and found possessions--Fiction. 2. Friendship--Fiction. 3. Toys--Fiction.]
I. Hefferan, Rob, ill. II. Title.

PZ7.K83692 Tq 2003
[E]—dc21   2002029389

Zack couldn't find Bronto! How could
a bright green dinosaur disappear?

Zack thought, "I'm big now.
I don't need Bronto."

But he still couldn't
eat breakfast.

When his friends came over, Zack said, "Where could Bronto be?"

"We'll help you find him," Henry said.

"That's what friends are for," Lucy said.

The friends looked around Zack's messy room.

"When did you last see Bronto?" Henry asked.

"He was on my pillow last night. When
I woke up, Bronto was gone!" Zack said.

"Maybe he fell in the hamper with your pajamas!" Lucy said.

But Bronto was not in the hamper.

"I clean up when things get lost,"
Henry said.

"We can play a clean-up game! See how
much you can pick up before someone
yells STOP," Lucy said.

The friends grabbed dirty clothes, books, and toys as fast as they could.

Then, suddenly, Lucy yelled, "STOP!"

Zack found five cents and a yo-yo.

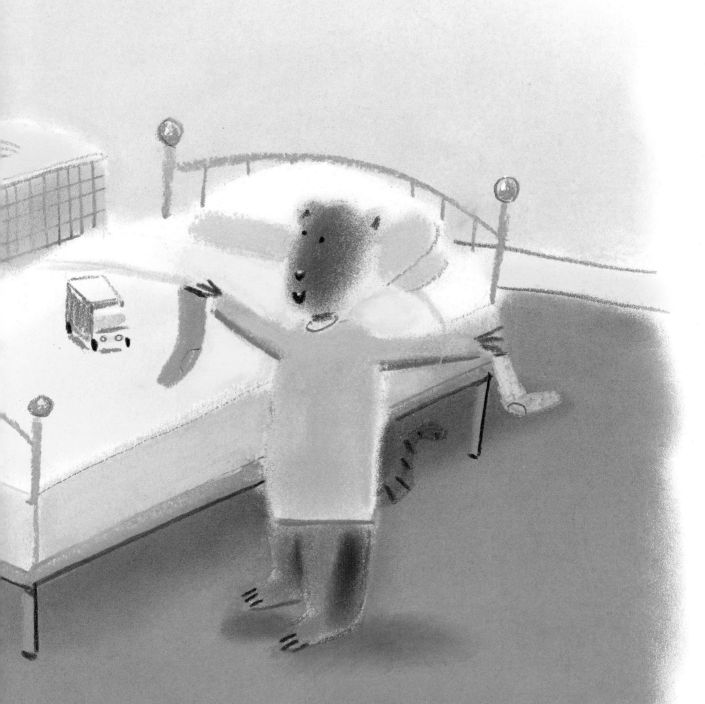

Henry found some socks and a red truck.
But they still hadn't found Bronto.

Lucy could tell Zack felt sad. "Let's play follow-the-leader!" she said.

Lucy marched down the street to her house.

Lucy marched into her room.
Henry and Zack marched in after her.

Lucy handed Zack her favorite bedtime toy. "You can have Power Pixie. She fights nightmares!" she said.

"You can have my football pillow!" Henry said. He wanted to be a good friend, too. "Follow the leader!"

Henry jumped all the way to his house.

Henry gave Zack his fuzzy,
brown football pillow.

Now it was Zack's turn to lead. "Follow the leader!" he said. Zack hopped home with the toys. Lucy and Henry hopped after him.

Soon it was time for Lucy and Henry to go home.

Lucy felt afraid of a night without her Power Pixie. Henry looked sadly at his football pillow.

Zack gave back the toys. "If you can sleep without your toys, so can I," he said.

"You're very brave," Lucy told Zack.

Zack smiled. "If I get scared, I'll just think of you!"

That night, Zack felt a lump in his pillowcase.
It was Bronto! Zack laughed. He couldn't wait
to tell his friends the funny news.